MW00783979

Silent Fright

13-Digit ISBN: 978-1-40034-707-0
10-Digit ISBN: 1-40034-707-6

This book may be ordered by mail from the publisher. Please include $5.99 for postage and handling. Please support your local bookseller first!

Books published by Cider Mill Press Book Publishers are available at special discounts for bulk purchases in the United States by corporations, institutions, and other organizations. For more information, please contact the publisher.

Cider Mill Press Book Publishers
"Where good books are ready for press"
501 Nelson Place
Nashville, Tennessee 37214

cidermillpress.com

Typography: Aria Text, Gandur New
Title vectors used under official license from Shutterstock.com

Printed in the United States of America

24 25 26 27 28 VER 5 4 3 2 1
First Edition

A VERY MERRY SCARY SILENT FRIGHT

CHRISTMAS COLORING BOOK

CIDER MILL PRESS

BOOK PUBLISHERS

SILENT FRIGHT SILENT FRIGHT

IGHT SILENT FRIGHT SILENT FRIGHT SILENT FRIGHT
IGHT SILENT FRIGHT SILENT FRIGHT SILENT FRIGHT
IGHT SILENT FRIGHT SILENT FRIGHT SILENT FRIGHT
IGHT SILENT FRIGHT SILENT FRIGHT SILENT FRIGHT
IGHT SILENT FRIGHT SILENT FRIGHT SILENT FRIGHT
IGHT SILENT FRIGHT SILENT FRIGHT SILENT FRIGHT
IGHT SILENT FRIGHT SILENT FRIGHT SILENT FRIGHT
IGHT SILENT FRIGHT SILENT FRIGHT SILENT FRIGHT
IGHT SILENT FRIGHT SILENT FRIGHT SILENT FRIGHT
IGHT SILENT FRIGHT SILENT FRIGHT SILENT FRIGHT
IGHT SILENT FRIGHT SILENT FRIGHT SILENT FRIGHT

WARNING:
THIS IS NOT YOUR TYPICAL CHRISTMAS COLORING BOOK.

Greetings, brave soul, and welcome to a yuletide season like no other. You won't find dancing sugar plums and jolly old Saint Nick here. These grim illustrations blend festive cheer with haunting horror. Prepare to encounter 50 ghoulish depictions of beloved holiday characters, from sinister snowmen and skeletal reindeer to creepy carolers and spooky specters.

These coloring pages are ideal for horror enthusiasts or anyone looking to de-stress with a uniquely unsettling twist. Each page invites you to reinterpret Christmas through a lens of terror, offering a creative escape from the conventional holiday hustle and bustle.

Dare to bring these eerie visions to life with *Silent Fright*. May your days be merry and macabre!

68 Silent Fright

SILENT FRIGHT SILENT FRIGHT SILENT FRIGHT SILENT
SILENT FRIGHT SILENT FRIGHT SILENT FRIGHT SILE
SILENT FRIGHT SILENT FRIGHT SILENT FRIGHT SILE
SILENT FRIGHT SILENT FRIGHT SILENT FRIGHT SILE
SILENT FRIGHT SILENT FRIGHT SILENT FRIGHT SILE
SILENT FRIGHT SILENT FRIGHT SILENT FRIGHT SILE
SILENT FRIGHT SILENT FRIGHT SILENT FRIGHT SILE
SILENT FRIGHT SILENT FRIGHT SILENT FRIGHT SILE
SILENT FRIGHT SILENT FRIGHT SILENT FRIGHT SILE
SILENT FRIGHT SILENT FRIGHT SILENT FRIGHT SILE
SILENT FRIGHT SILENT FRIGHT SILENT FRIGHT SILE
SILENT FRIGHT SILENT FRIGHT SILENT FRIGHT SILE
SILENT FRIGHT SILENT FRIGHT SILENT FRIGHT SILE

SILENT FRIGHT SILENT FRIGHT SILENT FRIGHT SILENT FRIGHT
SILENT FRIGHT SILENT FRIGHT SILENT FRIGHT SILENT FRIGHT
SILENT FRIGHT SILENT FRIGHT SILENT FRIGHT SILENT FRIGHT
SILENT FRIGHT SILENT FRIGHT SILENT FRIGHT SILENT FRIGHT
SILENT FRIGHT SILENT FRIGHT SILENT FRIGHT SILENT FRIGHT
SILENT FRIGHT SILENT FRIGHT SILENT FRIGHT SILENT FRIGHT
SILENT FRIGHT SILENT FRIGHT SILENT FRIGHT SILENT FRIGHT
SILENT FRIGHT SILENT FRIGHT SILENT FRIGHT SILENT FRIGHT
SILENT FRIGHT SILENT FRIGHT SILENT FRIGHT SILENT FRIGHT
SILENT FRIGHT SILENT FRIGHT SILENT FRIGHT SILENT FRIGHT
SILENT FRIGHT SILENT FRIGHT SILENT FRIGHT SILENT FRIGHT

ABOUT CIDER MILL PRESS BOOK PUBLISHERS

Good ideas ripen with time. From seed to harvest, Cider Mill Press brings fine reading, information, and entertainment together between the covers of its creatively crafted books. Our Cider Mill bears fruit twice a year, publishing a new crop of titles each spring and fall.

CIDER MILL PRESS

BOOK PUBLISHERS

"Where Good Books Are Ready for Press"
501 Nelson Place
Nashville, Tennessee 37214

cidermillpress.com